ONE
HORSE

Michael
Hardcastle

A Dolphin
Paperback

Published in paperback in 1995
by Orion Children's Books
a division of The Orion Publishing Group Ltd
Orion House
5 Upper St Martin's Lane
London WC2H 9EA

First published in Great Britain in 1993
by Dent Children's Books

Typeset by Deltatype Ltd, Ellesmere Port, Cheshire
Printed in Great Britain by Clays Ltd, St Ives plc.

A catalogue record for this book is available from
the British Library

ISBN 1 85881 106 6

**This book is to be returned on or before
the last date stamped below.**

t. 11. 99

ONE

Holly ran her hand down Gunflint's nose as the handsome grey horse jerked his neck up and down again and again. His coat dark with sweat, he was still excited by his exertions in the three-mile hurdle race. Holly reached back to tug the rug over his withers to prevent his catching a chill when they left the racecourse stables.

'Look, it wasn't your fault, it really wasn't,' she told him soothingly, waiting for her father to return with the news that their horsebox was ready for the journey home. 'You did your best, Flinty, your very best. You always do, don't you?'

The hurdler jerked his head upwards again, more fiercely this time, rolling his eyes, suddenly disturbed even more by a blast of unfamiliar noise out in the yard. Someone had switched on a portable radio but with so much interference on the air waves it just made a racket.

'That's diabolical!' exclaimed Holly. It was a favourite expression and it certainly fitted the occasion. 'Take no notice, Flinty, settle down, settle *down*. Think about supper. I'll give you something special, promise.'

Gunflint didn't seem convinced. In spite of the softness of Holly's voice he continued to fret and backed away until he came right up against the rear wall of his temporary stall. Holly was afraid that he might forget entirely where he was and lash out, striking the wall and injuring himself severely. She wanted to yell at the idiot in the yard, ordering him to switch off his murderous radio. But a scream from her would alarm the five-year-old grey still more.

'I *know* you hate that noise – so do I,' she went on in an urgent whisper. 'You and I are, well, a bit the same, aren't we, Flinty? We're both loners, like it best when we're on our own or with just one friend, don't we? I mean, I like some people and you like some other horses, but not too many, eh? I suppose I like other horses more than you do! You *always* want to be on your own in a race, don't you? That's why you sort of sulked a bit when that flashy chestnut bumped you at the fifth hurdle. Didn't want to know after that, did you? And Billy Wooldale didn't help, either. Giving you those whacks with his horrible whip. Maybe he thinks nobody noticed because it happened a long way from the stands, but I noticed. Hope Dad did, too. Billy's going to get the same medicine before long, I hope.'

Gunflint was no longer trembling so badly. He appeared to be responding to Holly's calming tones. And then, just as suddenly as it had started, the radio blare ended.

'Thank heaven for that,' Holly breathed, rubbing some of the horse's sweat from her face with the sleeve of her ancient anorak. 'Maybe we can have a bit of peace now. Don't worry, Flinty, we'll soon have you back in your own cosy box, all rugged up and comfy and not a thing in the world to worry about. You won't be racing again for, oh, at least a week. No, no, I'm only joking! Two weeks at least and then—'

She broke off, silenced by the arrival of her father. He marched into the stall in his usual brisk manner, automatically scrutinizing his horse. The scowl that threatened to become a permanent expression was still on her father's face, Holly noted ruefully.

'Still stirred up, is he?' Patrick Hill commented brusquely. 'Pity he can't manage to get stirred up when he needs to during a race. I knew it was a waste of time and money bringing him here today. Useless beast!'

'Dad, he's not! He *always* tries his best. Just needs a bit of time, that's all. Honestly, I—'

'Time we haven't got. You should know that by now. And his owner hasn't got any more time to give him, I'm sure of that. After what we've just seen this one do, I'm pretty sure Fitzroy Longwood has no time at all for him. Like every other owner I've ever known, Longwood wants results – and fast. He certainly won't think much of today's performance, I can tell you.'

'But it wasn't Flinty's fault,' protested Holly as her father went to check on the rug fastenings and collect sponge and bucket and brushes. 'You agreed when we watched the race together that Billy Wooldale had him all wrong at that hurdle, he didn't give Flinty a chance, he didn't give him time to get over that little stumble and—'

'Oh, Holly, I don't want to hear any more excuses. I've had enough excuses and I'm fed up right up to here with them.' The trainer drew a stubby forefinger across his throat. 'The owners are fed up with excuses, even more than I am, I expect. Come on, let's be off. Got everything?'

'Er, I think so,' agreed Holly, casting a quick look round the stall with its chewed doorpost and tangy straw. She knew that Gunflint's own box at Marshmoor Stables wasn't even three-star accommodation, let alone luxurious, but at least it was home. He'd be happy to be back there – and so would she. This was going to be another forgettable day at the races.

3

Gunflint was still moving nervously, and plainly ready to back off if the slightest thing upset him, as Patrick Hill led him from the racecourse stables and across a narrow metalled road to the area where all the travelling boxes were parked in rather untidy rows. There was never any difficulty in spotting theirs.

Holly regularly had a sense of shame as she saw the antique, wood-panelled construction on four wheels – complete with scratched sides and rusty hinges – that passed for their box. Someone had once remarked to her that it must be a collector's item because 'surely they pensioned off boxes like that last *century*!' She'd laughed because it was the only possible response to cover her embarrassment. She'd even offered to paint the box but her father insisted they couldn't even afford to buy the paint. Her other idea was to use some of the wooden panels for advertising – that would bring *in* some money. Her father demolished that, too: 'Who'd ever want to advertise with us – unless it was a knacker's yard? Come to think of it, that's pretty much what we are, anyway.' It was about the only attempt at a joke she'd heard him make.

'Had a good day, Paddy?' called a man in a dark green jacket that looked newly waxed. He, too, was leading a horse, a chestnut with three white socks, a winner in any company.

'What d'you think?' Mr Hill replied morosely, barely even glancing in the other trainer's direction.

'Ah well, there's always another day, you know,' the man replied, in the manner of someone on whom the sun always shone. He tipped his trilby at Holly who, charmed by the gesture, waved back. There were plenty of trainers who treated everyone as rudely as possible because they were arrogant and

4

used to getting their own way in everything they did. Dad, however, usually had little to say to anyone and his family generously said that was because he had a lot on his mind.

Gunflint visibly relaxed as he reached the box that was so familiar to him. All the same, sometimes he played up and was reluctant to enter. Not this time. The moment the ramp touched the ground he scrambled up it and into what he regarded as a safe haven.

'Well done, well done,' Holly praised him, turning him carefully so that he'd have maximum protection on the lengthy journey to Salterby and then rewarding him with half an apple. The other half was for her because all she'd managed for lunch was a cheese sandwich and half a bar of chocolate. Breakfast, eaten on the move in the gloom of a winter morning, seemed a lifetime ago. Whenever she arrived home after a day at the races she felt she could eat an entire banquet by herself.

'Take care, Flinty – see you soon,' she told the grey before slipping out of the box and into the cab to sit beside her father, who was already in the driving seat.

'All right?' he inquired as he kept pressing the starter before the engine fired.

'I think so,' she smiled, deciding it wasn't worth mentioning that Gunflint hadn't started to pick at his hay before she left him. The old box was often a problem to start and she wasn't going to distract her dad. This time, though, the whirring went on and on and she began to wonder whether they'd be able to drive home after all. If only they had enough money to buy a new box, a shiny, completely-up-to-date, utterly reliable transporter with power steering and luxurious accommodation for the humans as well as the horses. If only . . .

5

'Dratted thing!' Paddy Hill muttered, as much to himself as to Holly. 'That Raymond can never get it right. Don't know what I go on paying the garage for.'

'Oh come on, Dad, be fair! Raymond's just an ordinary mechanic, you know, he's not a genius. And you're not exactly giving him a Rolls Royce to work on, are you? At least he keeps us on the road.'

'How long for I wouldn't like to bet. I tell you this, if I had the money, we wouldn't be going to Raymond for our servicing. If . . .'

Holly sighed inwardly and waited for the inevitable phrase to be trotted out. Whenever her father was in this mood, it was always the same. 'If I had one good horse, one horse that'd win races and decent prize-money and really put us on the racing map. That's all any trainer needs to put a stop to worries about vets' bills and feed bills and garage bills and saddlers' bills and rent and owners' promises to pay up promptly and – and – *everything*. One good horse. That's all. We could begin to live because I'd know how to make the most of it. I ask for nothing more.'

He'd been saying it as long as Holly could remember; sometimes, she actually said a prayer before falling asleep that *his* prayer would be answered. Vanessa, her sister, said it would never happen because the Hill family never had any luck – and never would. And she should know, she always added. Holly, though, didn't believe her.

They shuddered out of the parking zone and Holly crossed her fingers and hoped that they wouldn't have to stop abruptly to allow something to go ahead of them because probably it'd be impossible to get going again.

'You know, we must look like a kangaroo. Well, that's what it feels like in here,' she remarked lightly, hoping her father might at least grin even if he couldn't laugh. She should have known better.

'Glad you think it's funny,' he replied grimly. 'You won't, though, when you have to drive a box of this age. You'll wish you'd never set eyes on a darned horse in all your life, believe me.'

To Holly's relief, their jerky progress changed to a smoother ride, although she thought she detected unusual clankings somewhere. If her father hadn't looked so grim she'd have suggested checking that Gunflint wasn't upset by anything. He was a nervous traveller at the best of times. But her father wouldn't want to stop now for anything short of a dire emergency.

Music would have been welcome to improve the atmosphere in the cab but, naturally, the vehicle was not equipped with radio; and Holly wasn't allowed to take her cassette-player to race meetings because Mr Hill said she wouldn't be able to hear any instructions he gave her. One of these days, she consoled herself, someone else would drive the box, they'd return home with a winner and she'd sing at the top of her voice for the sheer joy of living. One day . . .

It was dark well before they reached the motorway slip-road. By then she had lost count of the number of transporters that had overtaken them with drivers flashing their headlights in cheery greeting to a fellow racegoer. Patrick Hill didn't deign to acknowledge them, although he knew many of the drivers personally.

Once they were on the motorway he put his foot down and the old box gradually began to pick up speed. Holly glanced at her watch for the umpteenth time and calculated that they should be home in another two hours or so. She began to plan what she'd do after putting Gunflint to bed, as she thought of it. The cleaning and grooming and preparation of his feed and sorting out his box she might manage to

7

finish in about forty minutes. Once he was settled she could have her meal. And then—

The loudness of the noise was astonishing. It began without warning, a violent, crunching, clattering sound filling the cab. It was impossible for Holly to tell where it was coming from; it seemed to her that the whole horsebox was falling apart.

'Oh my lord!' Paddy Hill exclaimed disgustedly. 'That's *all* I need. This is going to finish us off good and proper if it's what I think it is.'

Wide-eyed, Holly stared at him, her mind trying to grapple with the consequences of breaking down on the motorway. 'What is it, Dad? What's wrong?'

'Sounds like the big end's gone, I reckon – part of the drive mechanism to you.' He was leaning out of the cab as if checking the road beneath them; but in fact he was listening to the scraping, clonking, grating noises that filled the air even above the rest of the motorway sounds. 'Just hope we can make the hard shoulder before she stops altogether. Don't fancy unloading Gunflint in the centre lane of a motorway!'

'Oh no!' Holly pleaded beneath her breath. 'Not *another* family catastrophe!'

TWO

As the engine cut out Mr Hill steered the horsebox towards the hard shoulder, biting his lower lip fiercely with anxiety. There was just enough momentum left to take the vehicle out of the traffic and it came to rest just over the line separating hard shoulder from inner lane.

Noises now emanated from the rear compartment and Holly knew instantly that Gunflint, not the transmission, was causing them. The reverberations as the hurdler kicked out against the partitions were all too familiar.

'See to the horse, Holly,' her father ordered. 'I need to take a look at the chassis, see how bad things are.'

She couldn't believe Dad hadn't heard what Gunflint was up to; yet he plainly wasn't thinking about the risks she ran by trying to calm a frightened horse in a confined space. She didn't think about it herself for more than a split second, because all that mattered to her was Gunflint's safety. Those terrible sounds from the engine would terrify any creature, especially one so highly strung as a racehorse. Moreover, it had already been a bad day for the grey hurdler with a whipping following his collision with another horse during his race.

'Take care – don't lead him out whatever you do,' her father remembered to tell her before disappearing under the vehicle. 'There're supposed to be as many accidents to people on the hard shoulder as on the motorway itself.'

That was something she immediately put out of her mind as she climbed into the box, calling gently: 'Flinty, Flinty, Flinty – it's all right. Nothing to get excited about. Promise. Come on now, come on.'

She didn't really expect him to calm down at once, and he didn't. His eyes rolling back and sweat streaming from his neck, he was tugging with all his might at his halter. And in between those ferocious wrenchings he lashed out with his hind legs. Already he'd destroyed one of the partitions and kicked the splintered wood to the very back of the box. Holly's greatest fear had been that he'd be 'cast' down on the floor of the box and unable to get to his feet. In a situation like that a horse could panic and in his struggles to rise could do himself a fatal injury. At least that hadn't happened. Gunflint was alive and literally kicking.

'Come on, come on,' she repeated endlessly in her efforts to soothe him. Her presence should have helped to reassure him that the worst of his ordeal was over but the grey horse was still too distressed to allow her to take control. He did, though, stop kicking out after a few minutes.

Holly managed to get to his shoulder and she reached up to pinch the skin of his neck between her fingers. It was a trick to calm a horse she'd learned from David Quarmby, the vet's son who was at school with her. It didn't always work but she prayed that it would now. Gunflint was still tossing his head around with a fierceness that worried her. In her anorak pocket was an apple that she wanted to give him but that was impossible. In a state like this he might bite right through her arm if she extended it.

'Dad, I need you,' she whispered, and not for the first time in her life. He'd taught her to be self-sufficient – and much of the time she was. But she hadn't his physical strength, and strength might soon be needed if Gunflint didn't calm down. At the moment, she couldn't imagine how they were ever going to unload him from the box. Still, if repairs to the vehicle could be carried out on the spot, perhaps he could stay where he was until they reached home.

Suddenly, miraculously, her father appeared. 'It's hopeless,' he announced, climbing into the box but scarcely even glancing at the lathered horse. 'Hopeless. I was right, the big end's gone. We'll have to call for assistance.'

The overhead light was bright enough for him to notice something. 'You all right?' he inquired. 'You look as white as paper.'

'Er, yes, fine,' Holly answered, not quite truthfully. She hadn't really recovered from the fear that Flinty might injure himself so badly he'd have to be put down. The surprise now was that her father was inquiring about her well-being. Normally she was always expected to fend for herself. 'Are you going off to find a phone or do you want me to do it?'

'That's my job because I can explain what's wrong. But we're in a pickle here because it'll be ages before anyone can shift us – and take care of Gunflint. Is he going to settle, do you think?'

'Definitely, aren't you, Flinty?' She had to be positive in order to convince herself as well as her father. But her throat was dry at the thought of being left entirely on her own on the edge of a motorway while her father was away. If Flinty were suddenly disturbed again by noise or movement then he might go berserk. 'But hurry Dad, hurry. I mean, I don't fancy spending the night on a motorway. It'd be a long walk for breakfast and we haven't even had tea yet!'

'Right, I'll do my best,' Mr Hill said, turning to leave. 'But don't—'

He stopped in mid-sentence because he'd come face to face with a policeman wearing the peaked cap and yellow jacket of the motorway patrolman.

'Right, what's the problem here then?' he demanded.

'Big end's gone, that's what, mate,' the trainer replied matter-of-factly. 'No chance of moving ourselves. We'll have to be towed, I reckon. I was just off to the phone. Couldn't radio for us, could you?'

The policeman had removed his cap to reveal a head of steel-grey hair that contrasted with his youthful features. His interest had clearly been caught by Gunflint, now almost motionless at the far end of his stall. His ears were back and his neck was still wet with sweat but he'd stopped trembling.

'That a racehorse?' the policeman inquired, for the moment ignoring the question about his radio. 'I follow the nags a bit myself now and again. Don't get many winners, though.'

'Join the club!' Patrick Hill responded with feeling. 'Yeah, this is Gunflint, five-year-old hurdler. Made a mess of his jumping today and finished nowhere. Got to get him settled down in a proper stable soon, otherwise he may take off again. Bit temperamental, this one. Now, about that radio officer?'

'Oh, right.' The patrolman scratched his thatch and put his cap on again. 'We can get the breakdown boys here pretty fast but what about moving the horse? Can you send for another box from your place? If you back it up properly you'll be able to lead him from one to the other, won't you?'

'This is the only box we've got. We can barely afford to run it, so that's why it's in the state it's in.' Now Mr Hill scratched his own head. 'I don't know how we're going to manage for transport.'

'What about a neighbour, or another trainer who

12

could lend you a box? Must be somebody you can call on.'

Mr Hill shook his head. 'Can't think of anyone. We live in a fairly isolated spot at Salterby and I, er, don't get friendly with other trainers. Keep ourselves to ourselves, don't we, Holly?'

Holly nodded. It sounded rather pathetic, put like that, but it was true. Perhaps if they'd been more successful they'd have established good relationships with other racing stables. But when nothing went right for you people didn't really want to know you.

The patrolman concealed any surprise he felt. 'Well, we've got to think of something. Can't leave things as they are. I'll have a word with my mate, Kevin, in the car, see what we can come up with. But let's get the breakdown boys here.'

While her father was away with the police Holly talked non-stop to Gunflint, all the time wondering how they were going to manage to continue racing without a transporter. It mattered to her more than anything. In spite of their bad luck as a family, the lack of money and continuous worry of unpaid bills and the sheer drudgery of some of the work in a stable without paid help, she couldn't imagine any other way of life. Horses, whether winners or losers, *were* her life. One day they *would* find a horse that would change their fortunes for ever. One day Dad's wishes would come true, she was sure of it. 'But please don't leave it too late,' she regularly prayed to whoever was in charge of these matters.

'No luck,' her father announced brusquely when he returned a few minutes later. 'Jim, the patrolman, phoned up a local trainer for us, Hugo Richards, but he won't help, said he didn't want to risk our horse bringing any infection into his yard. Typical! So we've got a problem, Holly, a big one this time. As if you didn't know. At least the breakdown crew are on their way They'll be here fairly soon, which is something.'

'So what're we going to do, Dad? About Gunflint? About getting home ourselves?' Holly's heart was really sinking this time. She knew that Gunflint would become restless again. On a Saturday evening the traffic on the motorway was lighter than at other times but the continuous hum and occasional roar would bother him the longer it went on. And, like Holly, he was ready for a feed.

Paddy Hill shrugged. 'Don't know, but Jim and his mate are trying to come up with something. Nice fellas, I must say. Really keen to help. Makes a change in this life to find strangers who are actually on your side. Look, you go and sit in the cab for a bit. You've done your share, love.'

She accepted. It had been a long day and there was no sign of when it would end; and she was beginning to feel quite tired. So, after giving Gunflint a few more affectionate pats, she climbed out of the box and was just about to get into the cab when the grey-haired policeman emerged from the patrol car, its revolving blue light still flashing brightly in the gloom.

'Was just coming to see you, love. Could you sit in here with us for a moment?'

Holly was startled. What on earth could they want with her? To question her about her dad? Had he said the wrong thing? Did they suspect him of wrong-doing? Her heart began to bump furiously as she slid into the back seat of the yellow-and-white car.

Jim's colleague was talking into a mobile telephone as Jim explained. 'I suddenly remembered my daughter, who's about your age, used to be pally with a girl who lives round here, family with a big interest in horses. That's why they've got these posh stables. Kevin here's calling them up to see if they can help by

14

maybe taking your horse in for the night. All we can think of. What d'you reckon, Holly? That is your name, Holly?'

She nodded, impressed that he'd remembered her name from the only occasion her dad used it in his presence. 'I hope they can help because I don't think Gunflint, our horse, is going to be happy in the transporter much longer. He's not the best of travellers. I suppose it's a bit of a longshot, though, that these people would have an empty box we could use.'

Jim smiled. 'Keep your fingers crossed. You never know your luck. Well, sounds like Kevin's found somebody to talk to. If they can help we'll pass the phone to you because you'll talk the same horsey language, I expect. Oh, by the way, their name is Machell and I think the girl's called Rowena.'

Before she could respond the other policeman was handing her the receiver: 'Go ahead. It's the girl herself on the line.'

'Hello, hello, this is Rowena Machell.'

The voice was really quite musical and yet deeper than Holly had expected from a girl said to be about her own age. She gulped and launched herself: 'Oh, hello, I'm Holly Hill. We've broken down on the motorway and we've got a five-year-old hurdler in our transporter – my dad's a racehorse trainer, by the way. Well, we can't get home tonight and we desperately need somewhere for our horse to stay. He's called Gunflint and he's grey and he's pretty hungry! The police have been marvellous to us but they haven't got a spare box that Gunflint could use. But they just thought you might be able to help.'

She paused for breath, mentally crossing her fingers and wishing there were some wood to touch. Her head told her, though, that the chance of success equalled Gunflint's prospects of winning the Grand National in the next five years.

'Well, yes, I think we could manage that, Holly,' was the astonishing response from the other end of the line. 'We've actually got two loose boxes free at present so your hungry old horse is welcome to a feed and a night's lodging.'

Holly was so overcome with surprise that she could scarcely speak. The sudden glow in her widening brown eyes told the policemen what they'd hoped to hear; finding somewhere for a temporarily homeless horse to be accommodated was another of their problems solved.

'That's marvellous!' Holly told Rowena. 'Just marvellous. Honestly, I don't know how to thank you.'

'No need for that,' was the crisp reply. 'I mean, you haven't seen the place yet. You and Gunflint might not like us. Now, tell me exactly where you are on the motorway and we'll come and collect you. I know you can't be far away because that'll be why the police rang us. Perhaps the best thing is for you to put that nice policeman back on the line and my sister can get instructions from him. She'll be driving the box, you see. She's coming to the phone now. Sally, hurry up! The cops want to talk to you!' Holly could hear the laughter and another voice before Rowena spoke again. 'OK, Holly, see you soon.'

Holly handed the receiver to Kevin but her mind was whirling too fast to be able to take in his conversation with Sally Machell; in any case, it was no longer important where they had broken down because someone was coming to rescue them. Her first instinct was to rush back to tell her father the good news and to share it with Gunflint. But she supposed the policemen would have some instructions for them as soon as the phone call ended.

What, she wondered, was Rowena really like? She

sounded so assured, so confident about everything. Could she really be the same age as Holly, barely a teenager? How convenient to have a sister who would just drop everything to drive a horsebox to the motorway to help out complete strangers. Holly supposed that her own elder sister wouldn't have reacted so readily even if she had still been able to drive. But then, in the circumstances, Vanessa couldn't be blamed for that.

'Right, Holly, we'll go and see your dad,' Jim declared after a quick discussion with Kevin. 'Seems the Machell girls will be here pretty snappily so you and your old grey horse will soon be out of trouble. And me and my old mate here can get back to sorting out the rest of the motoring public!'

Gunflint, she was delighted to find, was quite calm and even picking at the hay his trainer had provided. Paddy Hill accepted the news about his horse's new quarters without comment, although he nodded a couple of times to indicate his approval. It seemed to Holly that he was still more concerned about the box than its occupant.

'Can't think how I'm going to pay for this thing to be repaired,' he grumbled. 'The garage don't want me putting any more on the slate. Then there's the cost of getting us back home . . .'

'That's what insurance companies are for,' Patrolman Jim reminded him. 'I mean, you are properly insured, aren't you?'

'Oh, er, yes, yes, of course,' Mr Hill replied, rather too rapidly for it to be true, in Holly's opinion. She thought it might be wise to distract Jim from any further questions.

'Is it a big place, then, where Rowena and her family live?' she asked Jim. 'And is it right in the country?'

Jim nodded. 'Big enough for a farm, I'd say. Mr Machell's the wealthy type, financial consultant or something of the sort in the City; think he bought the place as an investment, and to keep the older girl sweet. Mind you, I believe both girls are mad keen on everything to do with horses, so you'll be in your element there, Holly. Ah, looks like the Seventh Cavalry have turned up to escort you to safety, Mr Hill.'

He was right, but little could be done until the Machells' glossy, modern horsebox turned up a few minutes later and Gunflint was transferred to it. Holly had expected him to jib at being led out of his own box while traffic was whizzing past within a few metres of him. Instead, he was as placid as a pet lamb. Holly was almost disappointed to see that a total stranger could succeed so easily where she herself might have failed had Flinty remained in a bad mood.

But then, Sally had taken charge of him as she appeared to have taken charge of almost everything else, with Rowena just as efficiently acting as her second-in-command. It was perfectly plain to Paddy Hill that these girls knew how to handle horses and he was content to leave them to it while he discussed matters mechanical with the crew of the breakdown truck. Having received a phone call which Jim said they needed 'to respond to right away,' the police patrolmen swiftly departed.

'Maybe I'll give you a ring one of these days, though, to get the name of one of your winners,' Jim said to Holly with his farewell smile.

'There you are, good as gold, that one,' observed Rowena, blue eyes sparkling in her heart-shaped face. Compared to her sister, she was quite petite with shoulder-length straight brown hair and a very wide mouth.

'Wish he always was, but I expect he's tired and hungry after his exertions on the track – and our problems on the motorway.'

'Well, his troubles are over now, Holly,' Rowena went on in what Holly was beginning to realize was her usual confident manner. 'We'll feed him up – and you, too, of course. I mean, you will stay with us tonight, won't you? I'm sure Gunflint will settle down if he knows you're still around.'

Holly's eyebrows went up. 'Oh, grief, I hadn't thought about *tonight*! Not for myself, I mean. I was just expecting to go back with Dad and, well, be at home as usual. But we don't even know how he's going to get home, let alone what time. I'd better have a word.'

Paddy Hill seemed to be cast in deeper gloom than ever. Plainly the news of the vehicle's inner health was bad: and that meant more money to be spent, perhaps lots of it. To Holly he seemed to be only half listening as she relayed Rowena's offer to put her as well as Gunflint up for the night.

'Seems the best solution,' he agreed. 'These fellas have promised to see to the box tomorrow, even though it is Sunday. They say I can sleep in it overnight in their garage, so that's one problem solved. I'll ring your mum and sort things out with her about the yard. She'll be able to cope. Well, she'll have to.'

'So it's all right for me to go to Rowena's? Great.' Holly felt utterly disloyal saying it but she *did* want to accept the invitation, and get to know the sisters better. After all, they were being remarkably generous to the Hill family. 'I'll get their phone number for you, Dad, so you and Mum can call me in the morning. I mean, there'll be loads of things to fix up, won't there?'

He nodded. 'Right you are. Just write down their address and phone number for me so we know just where you are. I'll ring as soon as we can make arrangements to get you and Gunflint home. His owner'll want to know what's going on for a start, if he pops round to the yard tomorrow. Go on, then. Take care – and take nothing for granted.'

That had long been one of his favourite phrases but it hadn't yet occurred to Holly that it was the outlook of a pessimist. She gave him a hug and then dashed back to the gleaming horsebox.

'Come and sit in the cab with us, there's plenty of room – and then we can really get to know each other,' Rowena invited.

'OK,' Holly agreed, suspecting she might be neglecting Gunflint. But when she discovered she had access to the van itself from the cab, she stopped worrying. 'Listen,' she said as she settled in for the journey, 'are you *sure* you've got room for me at home as well? I mean, I don't want to take anybody else's place, you know. I'd hate that.'

Sally was easing the transporter out into the inner lane with the sort of care that Holly could only admire. 'We've got plenty of room,' she said. 'Masses of it, actually. We're glad to have your company.'

'But—'

'I mean it,' Sally went on. 'In fact, it was nice to have this trip tonight. It ended the boredom. So we're really pleased to meet you, Holly – oh, and your horse.'

'Absolutely!' Rowena enthused, squeezing Holly's arm. 'And now we want to know all about you. So, tell us. Don't hold anything back. What's it like, living in a real racing stable?'

THREE

Holly slid her legs out of bed, stretched luxuriously and padded across to the large double-glazed window that overlooked the Small Paddock (she'd awarded it capital letters after first glimpsing it the previous night). Inevitably, a horse was grazing there, alone in the furthest corner by a clump of trees that would provide ideal shelter from the winds of winter and the hottest suns of summer. A bay with plenty of heart-room but a rather plain head, he was, she remembered called Orbit Three and belonged to a local butcher whose youngest daughter hoped for success in show-jumping rings. Sally had been dismissive about the horse as well as the owner and his family. Sally, as Holly had quickly realized, was positive in everything she said and did.

Casually, Holly glanced at her wristwatch. 'Grief!' she exclaimed aloud. 'It can't possibly be that time!' But her instinct, fine-tuned by having to cope almost daily with early morning stable chores, told her that it really was after nine o'clock. The sisters had insisted, though, that she sleep as long as she liked because they'd take care of everything in the morning (which was now). After all, they'd talked and talked and talked until almost midnight because there was so much they wanted to know about each other; and with Mr Machell away on business in Zurich and Mrs Machell content to leave them to themselves, they'd done just that.

Holly hadn't really expected to have a large bed-room, or any room at all to herself, but when Sally remarked on the motorway that they had masses of space at home, she wasn't exaggerating. On sight of Hazelton Manor as the transporter glided down the drive, Holly had exclaimed: 'But it's a mansion!' Rowena grinned and admitted: 'Well, a small one, I suppose.'

Although she didn't want to dwell on how wonderful everything at the Manor seemed, Holly couldn't help comparing the Machells' lifestyle with the claustrophobic existence of her family at Marshmoor Stables, Salterby. Even her bedroom there hardly seemed to be her own because it was crammed with such items as a broken-down sewing machine that her dad promised to repair one day and cartons of form books and racing records that no one would ever read again but which hadn't to be thrown away. Because of the isolation of Marshmoor, she rarely had friends over, which, she confessed to Rowena and Sally, was just as well 'as it's really embarrassing to show people that you sleep in something no bigger than a shoe-box!'

'But aren't your friends *excited* at the chance to look round a real racing stable and give apples and Polo mints and things to *winners*?' Rowena inquired as the three of them lolled on sofas and sipped delicious hot chocolate after supper.

'Well, maybe, if we had lots of winners and our horses won races on TV and we were *famous*,' Holly agreed with one of her lop-sided grins, put on whenever she talked with wry amusement about her family's fortunes. 'But a total of precisely one winner in two-and-a-half seasons doesn't impress anyone, does it?'

'So *that*'s why we hadn't heard of you before tonight!' Sally said with mock sarcasm.

'Well, you're not into racing much, are you? From what you said you go in for show-jumping and eventing and sort of just looking after horses for other people who've not got their own stables. So—'

'Not *quite* true, Holly,' Sally interrupted. 'We're quite interested in racing and in fact we've got a horse at present that's been over the jumps – point-to-point fences, that is. We're not sure what's going to happen to him. Trouble is, he really lives up to his name, which just happens to be Puzzle.'

'Why, what's wrong with him?' Holly immediately wanted to know.

'You can find out for yourself tomorrow, if you like,' was the answer. 'We'll be interested in your opinion, won't we, Ro?'

'Sure thing. We need to find somebody who can sort him out, otherwise . . .'

On that intriguing note, the talk about the mysterious Puzzle had abruptly come to an end as Sally declared that it was time for bed for those who had to get up early to work in the morning. 'But you lie in as long as you want, Holly,' she added. 'You've had a tough day. Ro and I will look after Gunflint for you, give him his breakfast and spruce him up – and we'll also field any phone messages for you. No, no, don't protest! Don't look a gift horse in the mouth, as the old folks say.'

All the same, Holly reflected now, as she took a rapid but revitalizing shower in the bathroom attached to her bedroom, she hadn't expected to sleep as long as this. The sisters would think she was the world's laziest stable girl, unfit to be trusted with horses used to their own early morning routine. On the other hand, it was comforting to remember they'd insisted on doing her jobs for her because they wanted to show how welcome she was in their home.

She was surprised, when she reached the kitchen, to find it completely deserted, although a place had been laid for one person's breakfast on the huge, scrubbed, farmhouse-style table. Holly didn't linger: her greatest need was to find out how Flinty had fared overnight in a strange box, even though he had seemed to settle well. She was sure he'd feel she'd abandoned him by now, so she wanted to reassure him immediately.

Even in the yard there was no one to be seen as she headed for Flinty's box at the far end of the long row. But then, as she caught sight of the horse rubbing his neck slowly against the door-frame of a different box, she came to a full stop.

He was a grey, a darker grey than Gunflint, with an unusual browny-red colouring that made him almost a roan. It wasn't just the beauty of his head that riveted Holly's attention: it was the look in his eye, the eye of a conqueror, taking everything in, bold and intelligent. He stopped rubbing and returned Holly's stare with the same intensity.

'Oh *yes*,' she whispered to herself. 'Oh yes. You are *somebody*, somebody I want to know. So who are you?'

She moved closer to read his name in the little slot beside the stable door, the manner in which all the occupants of the boxes at Hazelton Manor were identified.

'Puzzle! Oh, so you're the one they talked about last night. I should have guessed, shouldn't I? Anybody in the world could see you're special.'

Holly was about to reach out to stroke his neck when Sally came round the corner from the smaller block that contained tack room and feed room. 'Oh, hi,' she called cheerily. 'So you've found our mystery horse already, have you?'

'What's mysterious about him?' Unlike many

24

horses, he hadn't pulled away at the approach of her hand. Instead, he remained motionless as she stroked the handsome coat.

'His name, for a start!' Sally laughed. 'Because that's his sire: he's by Mysterious out of Who Knows, so he's pretty well named, isn't he? And, as we said last night, we never quite know what he might do next. Listen, I'm impressed you remembered our mentioning him last night. At the time you looked whacked, ready to pass out at any moment. So how'd you sleep?'

'Terrific! Didn't know a thing until I woke up about, oh, ten minutes ago. Look, I haven't even set eyes on Gunflint yet. I've left everything to you. That's diabolical!'

'Rubbish! I told you, we're just glad to be of help. Anyway, not to worry: your old grey racehorse is fine, he's eaten up, there's a sparkle in his eye and Ro's giving him a nice old brushing so he'll look his best when you see him. Still it's good to have you here just to make sure he's OK.'

Holly was only half-listening. Puzzle was leaning down to her shoulder now, tugging at her sweater with gentle insistence. No horse had ever done that to her before, though she'd been buffeted plenty of times by heads swung unexpectedly or wildly when food or affection were in demand.

'Look, if you can tear yourself away from your new friend and have a moment for your old friend I'll prove he's in good hands,' Sally suggested, a note of surprise in her voice.

'Oh yes, of course.' Carefully Holly detached herself from Puzzle's grazing. 'See you soon,' she told him, moving away a little guiltily.

'Hey, this one sure knows the sound of your voice.' Rowena, brush in hand, greeted them as they arrived in Gunflint's box. 'His ears almost shot off his head when he heard you were around!'

After a comment like that Holly felt she had to make a fuss of the hurdler who looked just as much on his toes as Sally had described.

On the evidence before her she could certainly assure his owner that Gunflint really did appear to be well and happy and none the worse for his experiences of the previous day. Plainly life at Hazelton Manor Stables suited him – as, Holly couldn't help feeling, it would suit her, too. She knew that she and Rowena would get on well and she wouldn't at all mind responding to Sally's authoritative way of running a stable. It would be very different from her father's haphazard style, alternating between doing everything himself or leaving her to hold the fort while he disappeared for hours on end. It reminded her of something she should have asked about earlier.

'Has my dad phoned yet? He must've sorted things out at home by now, even if he's still stuck at that garage.'

Sally shook her head. 'We'd've told you if he had. You must be starving if you haven't had breakfast yet. I'm ready for some coffee so we'll have a drink while you eat, OK? If your dad rings, you can take it in the kitchen.'

Holly would happily have settled for cereals and a slice of bread but Rowena insisted on making porridge for her because, she claimed, it was 'the healthiest start to the day anybody could have.' While the porridge was heating up and the coffee began to simmer, Holly asked about Puzzle. How long had they had him? Where had he come from? Did his owner really care about him? What might happen to him in the future?

'Hey, slow down,' Sally laughed. 'Nobody's written a biography of him yet, so we don't know everything. Fact is, we don't know a lot, only what we've been told by Mrs Bedale, his owner, and our own ideas from the way he behaves. But we do know he had a rough old time as a foal in Ireland, and that alone could explain a lot.'

Holly, sipping orange juice, nodded eagerly to show she wanted all the details.

'Well, when his dam was feeding him she got an abscess on a foot and her milk just dried up. Puzzle was about a month or so old at the time and *he* became ill because he wasn't getting the right nourishment.' Sally paused and then added: 'To be honest, I don't think those looking after him were all that bright. Anyway, when a vet was at last called in it was touch and go with poor Puzzle and he was only saved by night-and-day hand-to-mouth nursing. The nurse was a local lady who just couldn't bear to see him suffer and she fed him on a mixture of glucose and invalid's soft food. And it worked. He's here to tell the tale – well, he would if he could speak, I expect!'

'It'll have made a difference to his character, bound to have,' Holly pointed out, smiling her thanks to Rowena for the bowl of steaming porridge. 'Could all be in his favour, really.'

'How d'you make that out?' Sally wanted to know.

'Well, there's this girl in my class, Sophie, whose folks split up when she was still a baby, really – her mum just walked out on the family because she'd fallen for another man. So Sophie was brought up entirely by her dad, even though she had loads of illnesses, all sorts of things, fevers, boils, always in hospital, a *terrible* time. There were times when she couldn't, or maybe wouldn't, eat. But – and this is the important bit – after her dad found someone else

Sophie just got better and better. She can't really explain it but she's the brightest girl, the brightest kid of all of us in our class. Brainy, beautiful, talented, everything. And she says she's so lucky now because of her bad start in life – and she got over all her troubles in her early years.' Holly blew on her porridge and than tasted it. 'Oh, fantastic, Rowena! This is really, really good. Anyway, as I was saying, maybe Puzzle's the same, maybe all his troubles are behind him and he'll become a – a *star*.'

'I like your faith in the future, Holly,' Sally smiled, 'but I think Puzzle had other problems after he came to England. I doubt he's got over them yet. Mrs Bedale picked him out at the sales for her step-daughter who fancied herself as a point-to-point expert. A bossy, stop-at-nothing girl called Giselle, wouldn't you just know it, but Mrs Bedale's story is that the two just didn't get along together. *I* think Giselle gave Puzzle a hard time of it and that's why he's, well, to put it politely, pretty unpredictable. I know this, if he doesn't take to you, then you've had it. He can go – crackers! Even at the best of times, he can be a handful. All down to that hard-as-nails Giselle creature, I fear.'

Holly slowly swallowed spoonfuls of the delicious porridge on which Rowena had poured a quantity of amber-coloured runny honey 'for extra energy,' as she put it. 'He seemed to take to me – at least, he was gentle and interested and he has, well, a wonderful *look* in his eye. I know that sounds a bit gushy but, honestly, he appears a very special horse to me.'

'You haven't tried to ride him yet,' said Sally, this time not smiling at all.

'Could I?' was Holly's instant reaction.

'Yes, of course you can have a go, if you want to. I expect you're experienced in coping with difficult horses, aren't you, living at a racing stable? You'll ride a lot of "work" – isn't that what they call it?'

Holly hesitated, trying to decide how much of the truth to tell. She sensed that the sisters were going to be important to her in the future, so she didn't want to mislead them in any way. She realized that they liked her, perhaps as much as she liked them. But would they think less of her if she told them how in-experienced she was as a rider?

'Well, I ride a fair amount, I suppose,' she admitted cautiously. 'Point is, Dad prefers to ride work himself or get a professional jockey to do it, even though that costs money we can't afford and owners don't like to have to fork out for. He needs me for all the other stable jobs so he can't risk losing me because of a riding accident. Sometimes, I think it's crazy because when you're around horses all the time you could get kicked or something and be put in hospital. At least if you fall off on the gallops you usually have a soft landing, don't you? But, well, after what happened to Vanessa he won't take any chances. So . . .'

'Was your sister injured in a riding accident?' Rowena asked.

Holly shook her head vigorously. 'No, that's the strange thing, really, because she used to work with the horses much more than I do. She was in a car accident, almost a head-on crash. My cousin was driving, being a bit of a show-off I think. Vanessa saw what was going to happen and tried to save herself by grabbing at the support bar above the door. But when the car rolled over her right hand was really badly hurt. Broken fingers, torn ligaments, awful really. She's still having physio-therapy. She's no real strength in that hand so that rules out trying to control horses. She got money from an insurance company as compensation but it doesn't make up for all the pain and lost chances of getting a job one day. Dad says it's just typical of our family's bad luck.'

She hesitated a moment, putting on a wry grin. 'We're terribly superstitious, like most racing folk, I think. I mean, yesterday as we drove to the races we got near a bridge just as a train was approaching it. I told Dad to put his foot flat down so we could go under the bridge just as the train was going over it. That's supposed to be really lucky, you know. But he didn't make it. Now if I'd been driving I'd've got us under the bridge when the guard's van was right above us. That's luckiest of all!'

'Never heard that before,' said Sally, smiling. 'I read somewhere, though, that green is thought of as unlucky in racing. Is that true?'

Holly nodded. 'A lot of people think so. Actually, the car Vanessa was travelling in – my cousin's – that was green. So Dad said afterwards she never had a chance of getting out of it without doing herself an injury. Another thing, racing people won't ever describe a horse as black, even if it's the colour of coal. It has to be called "brown", even officially on race-cards. Greys are OK, though. They're often regarded as very lucky. Not Gunflint, I'm afraid.'

'Talking of greys,' Sally put in before the conversations became depressing, 'are you taking up the offer to ride Puzzle? He needs exercising and from what you've just said you don't have to be superstitious to sit on him. Just adhesive! That's what my father likes to call it. So the word sticks!'

Holly was too excited by the prospect of meeting Puzzle again to enjoy the pun. 'Oh yes, I'd love to.'

'Right, well, if you don't want anything else to eat, let's go,' Sally said, jumping to her feet. 'Another of Dad's phrases is: there's no time like the present!'

As she followed the sisters into the yard, Holly felt a thrill of anticipation run through her whole body.

The excitement was still there as Rowena gave her a leg-up into the saddle and the three of them made their way to Great Paddock where, as Holly had already noted, some show-jumping style obstacles were in position for practice jumps.

She knew, the moment she took the reins, that Puzzle was different from any horse she'd ever ridden. His movement was like the flow of a river: easy, purposeful, serene. He'd jerked his head once as she reached for the saddle but he objected to nothing she did. Her father, who always knew what he wanted in a horse in spite of rarely finding it, had drummed into her: 'Look for a good mover. That's a prime clue.' It was.

Puzzle flowed into action the moment she asked for a response. It was in her mind just to canter him round Great Paddock once and then perhaps increase the pace on a second circuit. She was mindful of the fact that she didn't know the horse at all but had been warned that he could be difficult; moreover, he wasn't her horse, or even in her father's care, and she didn't want Rowena and Sally to think all she cared about was showing off. She wanted their approval, but that was a secondary consideration; the first was her relationship with the dark grey horse.

They completed the first circle in such silken fashion that the lure of the gate-like obstacle was irresistible: irresistible to her and irresistible to her mount. It was as if Puzzle wanted to show *her* that they were a partnership in thought and deed. He didn't need picking up. Shortening his stride at precisely the right moment, he launched himself at the white-painted gate. To Holly it seemed as if they were rising together into space, into another element through which they could float to the sun if they wished. It was the most astonishing feeling of her riding life.

As they touched down, with Puzzle effortlessly resuming his stride, the sisters spontaneously applauded them. 'Terrific!' Rowena yelled. 'You look great, the pair of you.'

For the sheer joy of the experience, they repeated the sequence. This time Puzzle jumped even more fluently. Holly wanted to go on and on, round and round, up and up, but that wouldn't have been polite in the circumstances. She pulled him up, so that she could talk to the girls, and he responded instantly to her command, so sharply that she almost tilted from the saddle.

'Wonderful, *wonderful*, Puzzle,' she enthused, stroking his neck. 'You're out of this world.'

'Well, he certainly seems to go for you, in every way,' smiled Sally. 'Never known him so *relaxed* – oh, and eager to run and jump. Thought you said you didn't do much riding, Holly.'

'I don't, not for my father. But for a while I did some exercise work at a top stable. That's the stable run by Nolan Fairweather. He's *very* successful with some great horses. Dad was trying to do a bit of business, trading, with him. But nothing came of it.' Holly felt she was saying too much, but she couldn't stop now in the euphoria of her first ride on Puzzle. 'I got on pretty well with Delia – she's Mr Fairweather's daughter, just a bit older than me – and she and I rode together. I was lucky, I once exercised one of their best horses, Gavotte. Super ride. So I suppose I picked up useful tips there.'

Rowena was looking at her thoughtfully. 'Nothing scares you about horses, does it?

Holly was startled by that suggestion. 'Oh, no, Rowena! That'd never be true. I mean, we've all seen things go terribly wrong with horses, haven't we? And everyone's a lot stronger than I am. I just, well, *expect* to get on with them. But *this* one . . .' She shook her head in wonderment. 'He's just from another world. Fantastic.'

'So you'd be happy to ride him in a race, then?' Sally continued. 'A real race, I mean, a point-to-point at Thirkleby?'

Holly really couldn't believe what she was hearing. 'Sally, what're you talking about?'

'Mrs Bedale, his owner, really wants rid of him. Her step-daughter's certainly never going to ride him again. But she's entered him for the Ladies' Race at Thirkleby next month just in case he can run and she can advertise him for sale. She can still do that even if he doesn't race. But if he does and puts up a decent show, well, so much the better. I gather there's some guy around who might just be interested in Puzzle for his daughter in the future. Anyway, Mrs B is leaving things to me to do my best. If you want the ride, Holly, you can have it.'

'Absolutely,' Rowena added. 'With our love. So come and stay with us again next weekend. We'll have an even better time then, I promise. You can make it, can't you?'

'Well . . .'

'Look, if transport's a problem, forget it,' Sally put in. 'We can always come and fetch you. We'll fix something, for sure. Please say you'll come. You'll be doing us a favour, honestly.'

'Honestly?'

'Yes, *honestly*! And how could you turn down a date with Puzzle?'

'I couldn't! OK, I'll get here somehow – and ride him in your race.'

It was the most glorious prospect imaginable.

FOUR

'Those colours are gorgeous!' exclaimed Rowena with another admiring glance at the jersey Holly was tucking neatly into her riding breeches. 'Scarlet and gold really suit you. And you'll be very visible all the way round the course even if you weren't on a grey horse.'

'Fire and gold,' Sally mused, handing Holly a neat whip that seemed to have been designed with lady jockeys in mind but which Holly herself had vowed she'd never use on Puzzle. 'Not a bad combination at any time, so they ought to be lucky for you – and for us. So make the most of any good fortune that's going, Holly. I mean, I won't mind having my name in the record book: "Winner trained by Miss S. Machell." Sounds good, don't you think? Might start being famous then!'

It flashed through Holly's mind that the same might apply to her dad; and he needed a winner much more than Sally did. In any case, all her hopes, as she stood in what passed for a parade ring at Thirkleby Point-to-Point Races, revolved around completing the course successfully rather than winning the race. Dreams of that kind rarely came true on a darkening, damp afternoon on a circuit she'd never even seen before today let alone ridden over. She was thankful for the sisters' company but she wasn't really listening to them as they awaited the arrival of Puzzle's owner, Mrs Bedale, whose racing colours she was now wearing.

35

'Nervous?' Ro inquired with a flashing, bright-eyed smile designed to proffer confidence to her new best friend. 'You're not really, are you, Holly? Go on, tell yourself you *can't* fail!'

Before Holly could reply, Mrs Bedale strode into the ring. A tall, fairly gaunt woman in her mid-forties, she was sporting a luxurious red wool coat with a trilby-style midnight blue hat and they alone made her conspicuous among the rest of the owners, their friends and trainers. Her glance at Puzzle, who was being led round by a young man Sally described as 'a good mate', was perfunctory; Holly was the real focus of her attention.

'So, you're going to put up a good show on this fella, eh?' she demanded, rather than asked, briskly shaking Holly's hand. 'Needs firm handling, my step-daughter used to tell me. Used to call him a tough nut to crack.'

'Well, I'll, er, do my best,' responded Holly, trying to ignore the sight of Ro's eyes rolling upwards in amused disbelief. She knew it was a weak answer but couldn't think of anything better. Sally had told her that Stephanie Bedale's sense of humour was non-existent and Holly could believe that now. 'Business-like' was the word that summed her up.

'I sincerely hope so. Sally, I'm relying on your recommendation of Holly as a capable rider. It's time Puzzle proved his real value. So, I'll see you all back here after the race. Good luck.' She paused, clearly having said all she was going to say to them, and her eyes strayed over the rest of the people in the ring. 'Ah, I see Major Fairoak's here. *Must* have a word with him . . .'

'Phew! Glad that's over,' Sally murmured, breathing easily again. 'Got eyes like bayonets, hasn't she? I know she always makes me feel pinned down even when I know I'm in the right and she's in the wrong! Sometimes I wonder why I bother with her.'

'Because you can't resist an interesting horse, that's why,' Ro replied promptly before turning back to Holly. 'Don't let Ma Bedale put you off. *I* know you and Puzzle are going to be a great team.'

Holly smiled wanly. She was beginning to feel the burden of everyone's expectations besides her own. Yet, less than a month ago, Sally for one, and probably Mrs Bedale for another, had been writing Puzzle off as a no-hoper. Since then Holly herself had thought about the horse like an absent boyfriend (though that wasn't someone she wanted in her life!). At home she'd talked endlessly about him, so that even her dad had begun to take an interest in the grey, in spite of his concern about his own grey, Gunflint, who was proving listless and in need of a vet's attention. Mr Hill was disappointed that Holly hadn't noticed the darkness of Gunflint's droppings which probably indicated that the horse broke a blood vessel during his race on the Saturday the box broke down. 'I expect you were too taken up with your new friends and your new horse to see what your old favourite was up to,' he gently chastised her.

That apart, the weeks at home had gone quite well – and quickly, it seemed to her. The box was mended satisfactorily at a reasonable cost, Fitzroy Longwood was so pleased with one of his business deals that he was prepared to overlook Gunflint's lack of success and was even talking of buying another horse, and she'd done well in two maths tests and received unexpectedly high marks for two 'true-to-life' poems from her English teacher.

Then there'd been the return to Hazelton Manor one weekend to renew acquaintance with Rowena and Sally – and, of course, with Puzzle. She'd spent

37

practically the entire visit either talking incessantly about horses, or riding the roan wonder-horse, as she was beginning to think of him.

She'd discovered that he really didn't care for minor obstacles of any kind at all. It was almost as if they were, literally, beneath his consideration. So when she wanted to pop him over something that was barely above ground he sometimes wasn't hoof perfect: a hint of a stumble was what she'd get, although he didn't actually make a mistake. He'd then give a solemn shake of his head as if to chastise himself for carelessness, a trait that to Holly quickly became endearing. Puzzle never displayed temper of any kind and it seemed to Holly that what he always wanted was a real challenge, the test of higher ambition, the sort of fence that a steeplechaser would face. He would take that in his stride, even with a touch of nonchalance.

It was Sally who spotted something that Holly could never have seen for herself. 'I think you should sit further forward,' she suggested. 'He's a long-backed horse, you know. So you're more mobile, more flexible, in that position. I'm sure you'll feel more comfortable up front too, if you see what I mean.' Holly agreed the moment she adjusted her seat: she felt completely at one with Puzzle. She didn't, though, make the mistake again of fondling his ears with a sharp twist. He resented that as he showed the first time she did it by throwing up his head and almost giving her a crack under her jaw. So, that weekend, she'd learned a great deal.

The return to Hazelton Manor for the second time had been made even better by Ro's invitation to share her room. 'There are two beds in case of emergency, so you're welcome to one of them unless you want to hide away all on your own.' How far they'd talked into the ight Holly didn't know, or care; but now she felt that he and Ro were the very best of friends.

'Come on, don't look so *glum*,' Ro chided her as the ignal was given for the riders to mount. She awarded Holly a hug and a kiss before giving her a leg-up into he saddle. 'You'll dazzle 'em all as you flash past *veryone* to the winning post!'

'I just hope I'm still in the saddle when I do that, hen,' Holly managed to joke in reply.

In truth, her original confidence was ebbing away. t was only after walking the course a couple of hours go that she realized just what an ordeal this was oing to be. Some of the fences were bigger than any he'd jumped in competition – and, for all she knew, he same could apply to Puzzle. She had no idea at all vhat he would be like when she asked him to run and ump at racing speed. He'd been wonderful in school-ng exercises but a real race might scare him as nuch as it worried her. 'A tough nut', his owner called iim; and, Holly supposed, she ought to know.

After hours of soaking rain, the course was lefinitely boggy in places and Holly had tried to dentify the worst spots so as to avoid them. Two of the ences, including the first, seemed to be lower on the anding side than on the take-off side, so extreme care vould be needed with them. The circuit resembled a lattened oval with a sharp kink in the back straight hat ran parallel with a main road. It was the finish hat was said to trouble everyone: a long, steady climb rom the final bend that was sure to take its toll of ired horses and equally tired riders.

As she jogged down to the start with some of her ourteen rivals it occurred to her that she hadn't hought at all about the opposition; it had been :nough to think about Puzzle and herself and what hey might accomplish. Somebody had mentioned

that a rather elegant chestnut called Remember M
was the favourite, and a hot one at that. His rider
Amanda Fairoak, was just as noted for her long black
hair but that was now neatly tied below her white
and-mauve cap. Momentarily, Holly's attention wa
caught by Goldminer, a well-muscled, almost je
black horse, whose diminutive jockey looked to be the
youngest in the race by several years: which wa
virtually impossible considering Holly's own age.

Inevitably, her keenest interest was in the only
other grey, a much lighter shade than Puzzle's, the
mount of Mrs Delaney, said to have more experience
of point-to-pointing than all the other riders pu
together. Certainly it seemed to Holly that she wa
relaxed, although she wasn't chatting or ever
exchanging smiles with anyone else. Blue Lightning
was the name of her horse and he was sweating u
rather badly, despite his experience.

Holly kept licking her lips to keep some saliva in
her mouth. She'd thought a lot about how to ride thi
race but she knew that her strategy would probably
blow away like a leaf in the wind once they were a
heading for the first fence. It was always so easy to ge
caught up in the excitement of the moment and reac
to whatever was happening around you. If they al
went like a cavalry charge her horse would probably
match strides with the rest unless she used all he
strength to restrain him. But would he let her? If i
became a test of physical strength alone, then he
would defeat her.

There was no time to think of anything else. The
flag fell and they were off. It was as she feared,
pellmell rush to the first. As Goldminer charged int
the lead, Puzzle was slow into his stride and Holly ha
to kick on just when she'd expected to be calling
'Steady, steady!' In extravagant style, Goldmine

soared over the fence with two whippy bays in close support. Holly had intended to keep to the outside on the first circuit but Remember Me was now on her outside and seemed keen to stay there.

Blue Lightning, aimed at the centre of the fence, rose directly ahead of them. Holly was in mid-air when she sensed rather than saw the disaster that had overtaken Mrs Delaney. Somehow Puzzle was turning sideways as he came down and it was then that Holly could see the sprawling form of Lightning, who had capsized on landing, hurling his rider out to the left. In spite of the flailing legs of his rival right in front of him, Puzzle steered himself to the right, so avoiding both horse and rider – and, as it turned out, leaving room for Remember Me to touch down safely and run on without hindrance between the motionless Mrs Delaney and the riderless horse now desperate to get to its feet.

Afterwards, Holly couldn't recall how she really coped with that horrendous moment. All she could think about at the time was that, somehow, they were still in the race. A crash had seemed inevitable: and yet Puzzle took all the necessary avoiding action on his own. She'd merely stayed in the saddle, looking ahead, not down. Naturally, they'd lost ground because she couldn't for some moments urge him to pick up his stride. Her greatest pre-race worry had been that they'd perish at the first, probably in an undignified fashion. How could you explain that away to your friends and supporters? There was no way. You'd look a fool and feel a fool – and you were a fool, whoever's fault it was. Mercifully, it hadn't happened.

She reached down to stroke Puzzle's neck. 'Terrific! You were terrific, Puzzle,' she told him fervently. Holly risked a half-glance behind them and saw that no one was there. She was in last place. At this stage of the race, that hardly mattered, although, of course, she didn't know Puzzle's capabilities. She had no idea whether he had the speed to catch up or the stamina to last out the race. All she knew for certain was that he could jump and take care of himself (and her, come to that).

Everyone cleared the second fence without any trouble at all and then, as the track curved to the right, there was a long run to the third. Puzzle was striding out easily but she wasn't going to ask him for any real effort yet; she wanted to give him time to get over that alarming experience at the first. Sometimes highly-strung racehorses reacted violently to pressure after a mishap.

At the third an impetuous jump by the leader led to his downfall and now Goldminer took command from Star Supporter, a chestnut with a star-shaped white mark between his eyes which gave him his name. The favourite, Remember Me, was in the bunch immediately behind the first pair. Holly had devised a plan before the race to stay on the outside of the rest of the runners so as to avoid any possible trouble from fallers; and she also wanted to keep in touch with the leaders so as to seize her chance if it seemed Puzzle could win. Now she had to decide when was the best time to try to catch up with her rivals. Even in a race as long as this one, it wasn't wise to wait too long.

Puzzle was enjoying himself; she was sure of that. Jumping with great fluency, he was plainly eager to get into the race, to catch and overtake his rivals. Yet Holly was anxious to conserve as much of his energy as possible for the final stages. It would be awful if he ran out of steam just when she needed it most. But this was the kind of dilemma that faced most riders during a tough race.

By the time the field swung into the straight for the first time, with another circuit still to go, there had been two more casualties and Puzzle had moved up so that he was no longer last. Holly was thankful because now that they were approaching the makeshift grandstand she wanted her supporters to feel that she was still in with a chance of winning. She could hear some of the excited cries from spectators as Goldminer soared high over the fence right in front of them; but Star Supporter, with a much lower trajectory, actually gained on his rival while airborne. Now they were neck and neck – with Remember Me cruising in third place, six or so lengths to their rear.

Holly glanced to her left but she couldn't pick out Ro or Sally or even Mrs Bedale; she didn't know where they were stationed but she hoped they liked what they saw. Puzzle was running and jumping serenely and she couldn't recall ever feeling so secure in a partnership with a horse as she did with this beautiful steeplechaser. Because that's what he really was, she was sure: a natural jumper, and therefore made for the racecourse. Whether he possessed speed and endurance she'd shortly find out.

Half-a-dozen strides later she almost found herself on the floor. As they approached the original first fence for the second time she took the precaution, as she thought of it, of giving Puzzle a sharp call and a slap down the shoulder to look out for himself. But Puzzle hadn't forgotten what happened the first time round – and this unexpected signal from his rider confused him. Taking off half-a-stride or so too soon, he came down heavily through the top of the birch, scattering twigs and broken branches all over the place. Alarmed again, Holly clung on for dear life, fearful that she was going to be flung from the saddle as her mount lurched and stumbled to regain his footing.

Once again, their momentum was lost, once again they slowed almost to a walk, once again they appeared to be out of the race. On the stand that was once a hay-cart Rowena's hands flew to her mouth as she watched Holly and Puzzle falter on the brink of disaster. She couldn't speak but tears were starting in her eyes.

'You diabolical idiot! Idiot!' Holly admonished herself when she realized they were not going to part company after all. Once again, Puzzle recovered his poise and, with an odd shake of his head, continued racing, almost as if nothing had happened.

It was another two fences at least before Holly felt she could take command again. Oh, why hadn't she been *sensible* and left the horse to overcome any bad memories in his own way? It was clear now that she had little hope of winning the race. At the very moment that Puzzle stumbled, Goldminer and Remember Me decided it was time to start racing in earnest. The favourite's forward move drew an immediate response from the black horse, whose tiny rider lacked nothing in courage. But that competition almost immediately put paid to the chances of their closest pursuer. Star Supporter tried to go with them, took off carelessly at the next obstacle, and landed somersaulting. His rider, like Mrs Delaney, was flung clear and, to her own amazement, got to her feet without a scratch.

With a fierce race now developing between Goldminer and Remember Me, the crowd began to shout for their favourites. At that point, as the pair headed for the final sweeping bend towards the home straight, the Ladies' Open was surely between them. Two of the other runners were obviously tiring, another had pulled up, and Puzzle was a very long way back.

'Come on, boy, let's enjoy ourselves, anyway,' Holly called softly, giving him the gentlest of urgings to lengthen his stride – and race.

He responded like a racing car whose driver has firmly pressed down the accelerator. Sweetly, smoothly, he flowed into overdrive and Holly was astonished by the speed he produced when asked. Already, within just a few strides, the gap between them and the leading pair was visibly diminishing. It didn't occur to her that she could still win the race: that seemed an impossibility. But she might, if they went all out for success, literally run into a place.

Even before they approached the second last fence they'd overtaken two runners so that now only Goldminer and Remember Me were in front of them. 'Go on! Go on, Holly, you can do it, you CAN!' Rowena was silently urging as, wide-eyed with excitement, she watched Puzzle close on the leaders.

Holly disdained the whip, she wouldn't even slap him down the shoulders with her hand: she rode him merely with hands and heels – and he flew, sharing her exhilaration, in pursuit of the pair to whom they were getting ever closer. Over the remaining fences they rose superbly, as high in spirits as in achievement. Goldminer, tiring rapidly and faltering at the final fence, was now barely a length in front of them. Remember Me, however, had gone beyond recall and was already passing the winning post to the screeches and applause of his supporters and backers.

With admirable presence of mind and unexpected reserve of strength, Goldminer's frail-looking rider managed to rally her mount to hold off the late challenge from Puzzle – and so, after all, Holly had to be content with third place. It was far, far better than she could have believed possible only five minutes earlier.

'Brilliant, brilliant – you were brilliant, both of you!' whooped Rowena, giving Holly a hug of congratulation as she slid from the saddle.

'Oh, if only – if only . . .' Holly exclaimed, beginning to realize what might have been achieved if she'd ridden a different race.

'Now, don't blame yourself,' remarked Mrs Bedale, coming up to offer her own praise. 'Considering you don't know the horse from Adam, you've done remarkably well, Holly. Could hardly have done better, in my view. You seem to have worked out an understanding already, the pair of you.'

'Er, well, perhaps he just likes the sound of my voice,' suggested Holly, taken aback by the fulsomeness of Mrs B's compliments.

'I expect he does after listening to Giselle, because she's got a *very* sharp tongue,' Mrs Bedale nodded. 'Puzzle can be difficult, we all know that. But, I must say, he ran fast and true like an arrow for you.'

Holly, charmed by the poetical sound of that compliment, seized her chance to say what was really in her mind, something she didn't think she'd dare to utter. 'My dad's terrific with difficult horses, Mrs Bedale. He's transformed some diabolical racehorses. Honestly, I believe he could turn Puzzle into a real winner.'

She stopped, fearful she'd said completely the wrong thing and, at the same time, ruined her own and Mrs Bedale's relationships with Sally, who had come to pat and stroke the head-tossing horse and so far hadn't spoken a word.

'Mm, mm,' Puzzle's owner mused. 'Sounds an interesting proposition, particularly as you, Holly, would be around to exert your beneficial influence. Sally, what's your opinion?'

Sally nodded vigorously. 'Seems good to me. I'll be

sorry to lose him but, well, the way he performed today was a revelation. So if he goes into training, well, who knows what might happen?'

'Right,' Mrs Bedale went on briskly, 'that's settled. I'll be in touch with your father, Holly, and suggest he takes a half-share in Puzzle, or find someone else who'd like to be co-owner. Then we'll see what this mystery horse can do in real racing. Under Rules – isn't that what it's called?'

'Oh yes,' breathed Holly, hardly daring to believe her ears. She wanted to hug Sally for her support but feared Mrs Bedale might suspect some form of collusion.

'Exactly! Now, you'd better go and weigh in pretty sharply or there'll be trouble. We'll discuss details later over a drink – well, a cup of tea, anyway.'

After giving Puzzle another congratulatory pat and exchanging conspiratorial winks with Rowena, Holly headed blithely for the marquee that contained the official weighing-room. Her thoughts, though, were not on the race she'd just ridden but on the next outing for Puzzle, when he'd be an inmate of Marshmoor Stables, Salterby, and trained by Patrick Hill.

FIVE

Holly dug into her coat pocket for another Polo mint and Puzzle snuffled it swiftly from her palm. 'That really *is* the last one I've got – and you've had enough, anyway,' she told him firmly as he nuzzled her for more.

'Look,' she told him as she resolutely backed out of his box, 'I've got to go to school, *got* to. Wish I hadn't but I can't get out of it, not even for your first race – or can I?' she added as an afterthought. 'Anyway, you'll do your best, I *know* you will. Whatever you do, though, come home safe and sound. That's really the only thing that matters.'

Automatically, he put his head over the half-door as she fastened it, but her last touch of him was with the tips of her fingers of one hand: lightly, lovingly, lastingly. Superstitiously, she decided not to say another word to the grey horse until they both returned home later that day.

'There ARE others in this yard, you know,' her sister's ringing tones informed her as Holly was about to dash indoors to collect her school bag. 'If you're going to give mints out, you should give them to every horse. Honestly, Holly, this blatant favouritism's got to stop. You know Dad doesn't like it – and I don't, either.'

Holly stopped, turned and treated Vanessa to a dazzling smile. 'But he *is* racing today – and we want him to arrive at Covenham in the best possible mood, don't we? Dad's always stressing how important it is for everyone to set off and arrive feeling good. And it is Puzzle's first ever race for us – and for Mr Longwood, of course.'

Vanessa gave a sort of half-shrug and then, in a familiar gesture, pushed back her shortish, streaky blonde hair with her damaged hand. 'I know all that,' she pointed out, 'and I want him to win as much as you do, but there's work to do for *other* horses. I—'

Holly couldn't believe it. 'Look, I was up long before you this morning, Van! I've mucked out three and put in fresh straw and water – and I had to wait for *ages* while Flinty had a pee that went on for ever – and then start again. I've soaked the sugar-beet and sieved oats and scraped carrots for *all* of the horses. And you're supposed to be the full-time employee of this yard, not me. I'm just an unpaid, idle, opinionated, prejudiced schoolgirl – remember!'

Her sister placed the broom she'd been holding against a wall and threw up her hands in surrender. 'Sorry, sorry, I take it all back! To tell the truth, I've a rotten head this morning and I feel like crawling to the bottom of a well or somewhere beyond human reach. Or equine, come to that. I do know you do your share – and more. I suppose I'm worried to death that Puzzle'll turn out no better than the rest of the no-hopers we seem to get landed with. I don't think I can cope with many more failures, Holly.'

She paused as she saw Holly shoot an anxious glance at her wristwatch. Then, in a warmer tone, she went on: 'Listen, I'm really sorry you can't go with us to see him run his first race. It really is a shame after all you did to get him here. Pity the race isn't on TV – then at least you could watch it that way. If it's good news I promise I'll ring Mum soon as I can get to a phone.'

'I'm *going* to see him race, no matter what. That's definite, Van.'

Vanessa stared at her disbelievingly. 'But how? I mean, you can't! Covenham's more than a hundred miles away . . .'

Holly was already on the move, heading for the gate into the yard. 'Can't tell you that,' she shouted over her shoulder. 'But I've made plans. So you look after him like a – like a favourite brother. I'll be watching you!'

The ancient bus that was on today's school run was waiting for her at the crossroads and the driver blasted his horn twice as soon as she came in sight, to galvanize her into rapid action. She obliged.

'One of these mornings I'm *not* going to wait for you, Holly-bush,' he remarked affectionately, engaging gear.

'Then you'll probably miss a winner,' she replied brightly, flopping into a seat beside Stacy, her usual travelling companion.

'That'll be the day,' murmured the driver, accelerating sharply and thinking that it really was a very long time since his favourite daily passenger had provided him with a profitable tip.

'So which of your four-footed friends was playing you up this morning, then?' inquired bespectacled Stacy, who was forever writing what she believed was poetry in her free time. 'Not the perfect Puzzle, surely?'

'Naturally not – but I had to give him an extra bit of attention because he's racing today. Couldn't let him go all the way to Covenham without telling him to be on his best form 'cos I'll be watching his every move from 3.20 onwards.'

Stacy frowned and adjusted the angle of her rimless glasses. 'Is the race on TV then? I didn't think they showed racing on Thursdays, except at Cheltenham and places like that.'

'Not the sort of TV you've got in your brilliant old bedroom, no. And that's why I need your help when I sneak off school a bit early this afternoon. You will, won't you?'

The frown deepened. 'Will what? I'm not getting into trouble for you, Holly, even if you are my best friend.'

Holly blinked. She hadn't expected a declaration like that. On the other hand, she was well aware that Stacy seemed too bookish and bleak in manner to appeal to many people. 'Well, it was a bit diabolical of Dad, really, to run Puzzle on a day I'm at school. But he claims this race is a really good intro for Puzzle into real racing, so he's just got to take his chance at Covenham. Well, I'm *not* going to miss it. Luckily, our last lesson is in the library with your all-time favourite teacher, Miss Faithful Fiction herself. It's my one bit of luck today. All you've got to do, Stace, is grab her attention if she starts to wonder why I've disappeared half-way through the lesson. But it's odds on she won't notice.'

Stacy really did admire Miss Flixton, renowned throughout the school for her oft-repeated phrase 'We must always be faithful to fiction', and so, as she pointed out now to Holly, she wouldn't dream of lying to her about anything.

'You won't *have* to,' Holly replied exasperatedly. 'Just use your brilliant mind to *distract* her if you have to. You know I'd do the same for you in an emergency. And for my family, *everything* could depend on what happens in this race. So, *please.*'

'But where will you be going to, Holly. I have to know that in case – well . . .'

'Tell you later,' Holly promised, jumping to her feet

51

as the bus braked to a stop outside the entrance to Harbour High School.

Throughout the morning and early afternoon Holly thought of little else but Puzzle's first ever race in the ownership of Fitzroy Longwood and Stephanie Bedale. Her father had, of course, been delighted to take the horse into his yard and Mr Longwood, who was enjoying a run of success in his business life just then, took a half-share in him with alacrity. He always liked greys.

Since arriving at Marshmoor Stables Puzzle had proved easy enough to train, according to Paddy Hill; but, unfortunately, he hadn't so far shown anyone else the flair for jumping fences that Holly knew he possessed. He was inclined, while being popped over the makeshift obstacles on the training gallops, to make quite elementary mistakes. No one doubted that he had *speed*: when asked to quicken, he did so most impressively. 'Bit like turning on a tap – he just seems to flow,' reported Billy Wooldale, who rode him in most of his work.

That was the best thing Holly had ever heard Billy say about any horse but she still couldn't bring herself to like the jockey; and whenever he was in the saddle she prayed he wouldn't resort to the whip in an effort to squeeze more effort from his mount. Her father was naturally pleased with Puzzle's 'turn of foot', as he expressed it, but, he would add gloomily, 'jumping is the name of our game – and this one hasn't shown much aptitude for that yet.' That was why he'd decided that Puzzle's first race under National Hunt rules should be in a hurdle over two miles, at the undemanding Covenham track.

'But that won't bring the best out of him,' Holly argued. 'He's got this terrific talent for leaping over *fences* and if anything goes wrong he knows exactly how to put himself right. Honestly, Dad, he's *wasted* over miserable little hurdles.'

'So you say,' her dad replied equably. 'Remember, we only have your word for it. He certainly doesn't show that sort of talent when he's out schooling. If he doesn't buck up a bit and prove he's as good as you say then Fitzroy Longwood will be complaining we've sold him a real dog.'

At lunch-time Stacy tried her best to find out what her friend was up to in the library lesson but Holly, chewing slowly on everything she ate to keep her mouth full, would reveal nothing.

Throughout an unusually tedious English lesson, which focussed on a long-dead writer who seemed to think that various animals could take over the world, her mind constantly drifted back to Puzzle and his prospects. If *only* she were five or six years older and could have ridden him herself this afternoon! With her in the saddle, he would be brilliant, absolutely brilliant, she *knew* it. She'd proved she could ride properly in the 'amateur' world of point-to-points, so why wasn't she allowed to have a go in 'professional' racing? It really wasn't fair.

'Holly Hill, you're dreaming again,' Mr Blackburn admonished her. 'Of horses, I do not doubt. Well, there are other quadrupeds – bipeds, too – worthy of even your attention. So, concentrate, Holly.'

'Sorry,' she murmured, and gave him her most dazzling smile. She was thankful that he liked her.

With Miss Flixton, in the final period of the day, she avoided such exchanges by slipping out of the library within five minutes of entering it. Her absence was hardly likely to be noticed because pupils were forever getting up to no good behind the stacks in the L-shaped room; and as long as there was no un-acceptable noise level the librarian didn't seem to worry. In any case, Holly was confident that Stacy, for all her protestation about 'twisting and mangling the truth', would cover for her. Miss Flixton always beamed on devoted workers like Stacy.

No one tried to intercept Holly, or question her destination, as, head down, she purposefully made her way out of school, down the drive and on to Harbour Road. Not for an instant did she slow down or look back.

Ray's betting shop was in Pier Street, almost in the town centre, but her luck was in because she didn't see anyone she knew on the way there. Because no one under the age of eighteen is allowed on such premises Holly had to sneak down a convenient alleyway to ring the bell at the rear of the building. As she waited for someone to free the special security locks and open the door, she kept glancing anxiously down the alley, her fingers crossed that no strolling policeman would catch sight of her.

'Holly! What an unexpected pleasure.' Ray Cable, the white-haired proprietor, smiled broadly at her from behind the half-open door. 'Have you brought me some exclusive information from your star-studded stable? How very good of you.'

'Not exactly,' replied Holly, returning his grin and enjoying, as always, his extravagant banter. 'We've got a runner in the 3.45 at Covenham and you're my only chance of seeing him in action. The race is being shown on the shop's satellite system, isn't it?'

'Certainly,' he replied, opening the door wide and beckoning her in. 'You're most welcome, as ever. You can see it on the screen in my private office, then nobody'll know you're here. Can't risk my licence, you know: not even for a girl as beautiful as you, my dear.'

'Ray, you're a hero – mine, anyway. I think I'd've gone mad if I hadn't seen Puzzle in action this afternoon.' She followed him into the office; but for the three TV screens set into one wall and twin steel safes in the far corner it would have resembled a comfortable sitting-room in a private house.

'This is a real dark horse of yours, is it, this Puzzle?' the bookmaker went on genially. 'I can tell you that up to a few minutes ago nobody's been in to put so much as five pence let alone five quid on your runner. Are they all holding back for a last-minute plunge at the best odds? Hope you're going to tell me, Holly, because I can't afford to lose a fortune today on a local horse!'

'No risk of that, Ray,' Holly laughed. 'Dad and Vanessa don't think he's likely to win and I've spent all my pocket money. Honestly, we don't know what Puzzle's going to do. I've just got my fingers crossed for him. But he'll win one day, I'm absolutely sure of that. Oh, by the way, he's not a dark horse in any sense. Actually, he's a grey. And—oh, look, there he is!'

She pointed to the middle screen where the camera was tracking the runners in the 3.45 at Covenham and, at that moment, was beginning to focus, as the commentator put it, 'on the solitary runner from the Paddy Hill stable at Salterby. Come a long way, this one, for his first outing over timber and not much is known about him. I can tell you, though, that he's by Mysterious out of a dam called Who Knows, and he's neatly named, whatever else. Probably needs this run to show him what the jumping game is all about. At his current odds of 33–1 there doesn't seem to be much stable confidence behind him. But he's got a nice head and a good stride, so could be one to watch for the future. And now we're looking at Andalusian, the probable outright favourite at the off, winner of his only previous race by a widening ten lengths at Wetherby. Could be a class above the rest and . . .'

'A *nice* head!' Holly exploded. 'He's beautiful – and he's got the best look you've ever seen. Like a – like king, a conqueror.'

'Ah, yet another young lady in love with a race-horse,' Ray Cable sighed. 'Happens all the time, you know. Now, Holly, I've got to go and see that my staff are doing their job and no one's trying to pull a fast one over me. You've always got to be on your toes in the racing game. The kitchen's through there so just help yourself to a drink if you feel like it. If I don't get back before the "off" I hope your beautiful horse trots up. On current reckoning, I should make a few quid if he does.'

Holly was perfectly happy to be left on her own; if Puzzle ran poorly she wouldn't want an audience for her grief. With still a few minutes to tick by before the race started she thought she might as well make herself some tea. While she waited for the electric kettle to boil she reflected on Ray's kindness to her. In a community as small as Salterby everyone knew practically everyone else, but she had first met him at the races with her father who loyally placed his few bets with the local bookmaker. She'd liked him immediately and Ray had remained courteous and friendly towards her and her family. From time to time she had exchanged items of racing gossip with him but this was the first time she'd ever asked such a favour. She'd been positive, though, that he wouldn't refuse her.

As the runners were led out of the parade ring and then released on to the track, it suddenly struck her as rather odd that she should be looking at her sister on a TV screen; it had never occurred to Holly that when she had led her father's horses round and round before a race that thousands upon thousands of people were probably watching her as well as the horses and perhaps speculating on who she was and how she managed to get such a role.

Vanessa could clearly be seen mouthing 'Good luck!' to Billy Wooldale and then giving Puzzle a farewell pat before, cradling his travelling rug in her arms, she made her way to the small stand where the stable lads (most of whom were lasses) could watch the race. The grey moved sweetly into his consuming stride and Holly's heart lifted. She knew exactly how Billy must be feeling and she would have given almost anything to exchange places with him at that moment.

A glance at the first screen showed that while Puzzle remained at 33–1 the favourite, Andalusian, was shortening all the time and was now odds-on at 8–13; second favourite was Sheer Madness, who proved to be a bay with two white 'socks' and a habit of swishing his tail fiercely all the time, something horses usually do only when they are alarmed or in pain. To Holly he appeared calm enough but she thought that any horse saddled with such an awful name was entitled to be displeased. The only other grey among the fourteen runners was called Pale Dawn and he seemed reluctant to take part in the proceedings as the starter called them into line behind the tape.

Holly's heart and nerves began to flutter. 'Oh, Puzzle, run well, but come back safe, whatever you do. And – and Billy Wooldale, if you hit him, if you hit him more than once, I'll kill you! I swear it.'

When the tape snapped sideways and the fourteen runners moved away, Puzzle, just as at Thirkleby, was slow into his stride. But he wasn't so slow that the commentator remarked on it. His attention was snatched by Sheer Madness who went off 'like a ball from a cannon', which seemed an outdated description to Holly. On the other hand, the tail-swirling bay really did leave everything behind him as he set the pace.

Billy settled Puzzle down at the back of the field and Holly thought that was probably the right thing to do until they'd jumped the first obstacle. But when they did jump, Puzzle rose so high that even the commentator remarked on it: 'Puzzle, the grey at the rear, looked as though he was trying to leap over the grandstand there! The Covenham hurdles aren't really as high as that, I can tell you. Up front, Sheer Madness is increasing his lead if anything and . . .'

Holly grimaced. 'Puzzle, don't be stupid. You'll waste energy if you jump like that – *and* you'll have no chance of catching the others.' His jockey delivered the same sort of message by slapping his mount sharply down the shoulder. Puzzle flicked his ears, shook his head – and cruised on at the same pace.

Pale Dawn suddenly made a forward move to close on the leader and Holly wished it were her own grey – because that's how she usually regarded Puzzle in spite of the fact that he was jointly owned by Fitzroy Longwood and Stephanie Bedale – who was going so well. On the other hand, it was perfectly obvious to her that the favourite, Andalusian, was going best of all with his jockey so confident that his manner was almost nonchalant. Although all the runners were classed as novices, none of them made a semblance of a mistake until a light chestnut hit the fifth hurdle really hard, stumbled on landing and unceremoniously unshipped his jockey. That seemed to spark off a whole series of jumping errors and Sheer Madness lost his lead when sprawling awkwardly after ploughing through the third obstacle from home. His rider somehow kept his seat but the bay's momentum was lost.

By now Puzzle was so far behind that Holly was in total despair. 'Go on, go ON!' she yelled at the heedless Billy Wooldale. 'He's got speed but he's not a Formula One racing car. Move up, move up.'

Belatedly, it seemed that Billy had got the message. Suddenly, his whip arm rose, Puzzle received a stinging blow on his flank – and the pair were off in pursuit of Pale Dawn and the other front runners. Holly, fighting back an urge to swear or kick something, watched grimly as the jockey drove Puzzle to greater efforts as they approached the second last hurdle, right on the heels of the horse in fifth place.

This time Puzzle didn't jump so high: and, unluckily, that was almost his undoing. For, as the wooden hurdle swung back into place after being kicked by the horse ahead of him, Puzzle was struck a sharp blow just below the knee. Momentarily, he lost balance as he touched down, skittering sideways until he righted himself. Holly's eyes widened in horror as she feared that he'd fall – and then closed briefly in relief as Billy collected his mount and even allowed him a breather before trying to resume the chase.

After that mishap, however, pursuit was really a hopeless cause. Andalusian moved up smoothly to join Pale Dawn in the lead and these two, well ahead of the rest of the remaining runners, fought out a ding-dong duel all the way from the last obstacle which they jumped in unison. On the line, the favourite got up by the narrowest margin, a short-head, to the immense joy of his backers. Puzzle, jumping the last cautiously, kept on at much the same pace to finish in sixth place. Billy Wooldale, realizing that they had no hope of getting into the prize-money places, didn't use his whip again.

'Well done, well done,' Holly praised him in a

fervent whisper; and then added: 'Considering the sort of race *he* rode on you!'

'So, what'd'you think of that performance?' inquired Ray, coming in with a half-smile. 'Not good for the poor old bookies, I can tell you, with that favourite winning.'

'W-e-l-l, not bad, I suppose,' replied Holly, not quite knowing what to say. 'For a first time over hurdles, I mean.'

Ray dropped into one of the armchairs opposite her. 'Better than that, I'd say,' he remarked reflectively. 'Once he started racing, he made up a lot of ground. He was really being ridden for speed in the final couple of furlongs but he needed to be a top-notch flat race sprinter to make the first three from that far back. But he kept on and his jumping improved almost hurdle by hurdle.'

Holly was amazed he'd noted all that, considering that he must have had at least equal interest in several of the other, better-backed, runners – and especially in the red-hot favourite. No doubt his powers of observation helped to make him a successful businessman. She felt greatly cheered by his impressions of Puzzle's abilities.

'So you think he could become a real racehorse?' she inquired cautiously, not daring to pitch her hopes too high.

'Oh, definitely. Handled properly, he should have a good future – should make up into a good horse.' He stood up, smiled and seemed about to go.

Holly jumped to her feet – and, to the bookmaker's evident astonishment, she kissed him warmly on the cheek.

'Oh, I'm *so* glad somebody else believes in him, too,' she exclaimed. 'Thank you for that – and thank you for letting me watch the race.'

'Any time, Holly, any time you like.'

'Well, the *next* time he runs I want to be there in person. I want to be the one looking after him at the racecourse.'

But, within hours, she learned that Puzzle might never race again while trained by Patrick Hill.

SIX

Holly was just on the point of announcing that she was going to bed when the phone rang in the sitting-room. The thought flashed through her mind that it might be Rowena to say that she couldn't come to stay with them tomorrow after all. But before Holly could dash across the room to snatch up the receiver, her father, foraging through some invoices and unpaid bills on his antique roll-top desk, picked it up.

'Oh, hello, Mrs Bedale, how are you?' he said, his voice lifting as soon as he knew the identity of his caller. 'You'll be wanting to know about Puzzle, I expect.'

Holly, whose heart resumed its normal beat when she knew the call was nothing to do with Ro's visit, abandoned her interest in the magazine she was reading. Could it be bad news after all?

'Well, I'm very sorry to hear that, Mrs Bedale, *very* sorry indeed,' Patrick Hill said after a long interval of listening. 'The horse is coming along really well after that bang on a foreleg in his first race. *Really* well. He's relaxed and ready to do his best, I'm sure of it. Holly here has been looking after him like he was her very own – you won't be surprised to hear that, I imagine. Gives him a pick of grass at the end of every morning exercise when she's out on the gallops with us. That always relaxes a horse, you know, tells him work's over for the day. That sort of—'

He broke off as Mrs Bedale interrupted his

enthusiasm. Holly couldn't remember hearing him sing a horse's praises quite like that before. It was almost as if he were trying to sell her the horse!

'Well, of course, if you've already decided to sell your share in him I don't suppose I can change your mind,' he resumed after another lengthy span. 'I must tell you I couldn't afford him myself – no, not even at a knockdown price. I'm a trainer, not an owner. I know Mr Longwood wasn't keen to have more than a half-share but I may be able to persuade him to take the other half now. But he can be very stubborn at times. I can't think of anyone else who'll be interested – well, not immediately, I mean. I'll try, naturally.'

He paused again, glanced at Holly and then swiftly looked away again to avoid the horror in Holly's eyes. Plainly, the conversation was upsetting him, too.

'I'm sorry, really sorry, Mrs Bedale, that you're doing this,' he managed to say finally. 'I'm positive that Puzzle will pay his way eventually. Anyway, I'll be in touch when I have some news. Good night then.'

Carefully he replaced the receiver and gave his younger daughter a wry, sympathetic smile. 'You've got the message, I'm sure. Our newest owner wants to become an ex-owner. Insists on selling her half-share for the best price she can get. An impatient woman, that's obvious.'

'But—'

'Don't say it, Holly! I know just what you're thinking and feeling. She's not the sort of woman who'll ever change her mind. I guessed that from the first moment I met her.'

He might have said more but at that moment Vanessa came into the room and sensed the atmosphere at once. 'Don't tell me – *more* bad news,' she said. Then she saw Holly's expression. 'Ah, and let me guess: it concerns little sister's personal pet, pretty boy Puzzle himself!'

Holly was too upset to take that. 'Oh *you!*' she exclaimed. 'You don't care enough for any of them. All our horses are the same to you. Well, I don't think they are. Puzzle is very special. *Anybody* should be able to see that.'

Then, without another word to anyone, she fled to her room.

Thirty-six hours later, Puzzle's fate was still dominating her thoughts. Since Rowena had arrived they'd scarcely talked of anything else. But then, Ro seemed to be as captivated by the grey horse as Holly was.

'So what *are* we going to do?' she asked for the umpteenth time, putting away dandy brush and comb and hoof pick and oil and the rest of the grooming equipment before feeding Puzzle a final mint.

Ro, rubbing the horse's nose and admiring the sheen of his coat, was thinking about something Holly had told her before they got up that morning. 'Are bookmakers allowed to own horses? I mean, your friend Ray sounds a nice guy – and obviously he likes Puzzle. So perhaps he'd have the other half-share. Nothing lost in asking him, is there?'

Holly eased them both out of the box, firmly closed the half-door and gave her favourite a farewell pat. 'Well, I don't see why not – just as long as they don't ride 'em in a race! It would be pretty tempting, wouldn't it, to drop your hands if you were on the favourite and thousands of pounds had been bet on it. It's a thought, Ro – I *could* ask him. On the other hand, Mr Longwood might not want to share with a bookie. Not everyone likes bookies, particularly if they lose money to them.'

'Then we should ask him how he feels and if he would be partners with your lovely bookie,' declared Ro, her eyes sparkling with thoughts of another adventure with Holly. 'If you've got a bike I could borrow we could shoot off right now.'

'Great! You could have Vanessa's – she hardly ever uses it nowadays. Let's ask her.'

Her sister was preparing a linseed and barley mash when they located her and Holly at once felt guilty; the food was going to be a treat for Gunflint, who was officially on the 'pampering list,' as Paddy Hill described the horses who were being nursed back to full fitness. Until Puzzle's arrival, Holly would have insisted on looking after Flinty herself. Tactfully, she avoided that subject and simply asked if Ro could use her bike.

Vanessa nodded. 'Of course. Help yourself. Going somewhere special or just sightseeing?'

Holly hesitated only for a moment. 'Actually, we're going to talk to Mr Longwood. Going to ask him about finding someone who'll take the other half-share in Puzzle. Probably a longshot but . . .'

Vanessa rubbed her forehead with the back of her wrist. 'I've been thinking. If things go really wrong and we can't find anyone else to buy out Mrs Bedale, well, I'm willing to put money in myself. You know I got that lump sum in compensation: well, all it does is earn interest in a deposit account at the bank. It'd be much more usefully employed helping to keep Puzzle in our yard. I'm coming round to your view, Holly, after seeing him on the gallops recently. He *is* full of promise. I think he's really beginning to enjoy himself here. I know my money probably wouldn't be enough on its own but it might buy, say, a quarter-share. So if somebody knew that and was interested . . .'

She wasn't able to say any more because Holly

darted forward to give her a bear hug of gratitude and affection. 'Van, that's fantastic! A wonderful, wonderful offer. But we mustn't use your money if we can help it. Just in an emergency, right? Ro, let's head for the Longwood Estate and see if miracles still happen.'

It was only when they were skimming down the rutted, leafy lane leading to the house itself that it occurred to Holly that perhaps she should have telephoned for an appointment. If the racehorse owner wasn't at home, or was too busy to see them, then it would be a totally wasted journey.

'Nonsense!' Rowena exclaimed when Holly confided her fears. 'This has got to be our lucky day because we're together after *ages* apart. And how could any decent man refuse to see two dazzling young ladies who've dropped in on him out of the blue with, er, an *irresistible* offer!'

'Of course! Holly agreed, laughing. 'Impossible to refuse.'

Fitzroy Longwood might have been listening into that conversation on a private line because it was he who opened the door to their ring which caused bells to chime. 'Ah,' he greeted them, smiling broadly and eyebrows shooting up, '*two* charming ladies on my doorstep. What an honour, what a pleasure. You, Holly, I know but—'

The introductions neatly made, he led them across a tiled hall to an office that was as modern as the house was ancient. It looked, to Holly's experienced eyes, to be the international businessman's equivalent of Ray Cable's bookmaker's sitting-room, with teletext screens in one corner displaying share prices and currency movements. The black desk was L-shaped and the chairs around a low table were of green leather and much more comfortable than they appeared.

'You will have something to drink, of course?' Mr Longwood inquired. Without waiting for a reply, he walked across to a glass-fronted cabinet and made clinking sounds with ice and glasses and unseen ingredients. Holly couldn't imagine what he was going to offer them but she hoped it would be acceptable.

'Ginger beer for you, something a touch stronger for me,' he revealed with a grin, handing over cut-glass tumblers. 'Now, dear young ladies, tell me what you've come about. I'll have a bet with myself and put my money firmly on Puzzle. He *is* fit, I trust?'

Holly nodded vigorously. 'Definitely. All the heat's gone from his injured leg and he's in terrific form. Even Vanessa says so, and you know she's always, well, a bit cautious.'

The plump, grey-haired owner smiled his agreement. Then, marginally adjusting the angle of his rimless spectacles, he asked the question Holly was dreading but knew was inevitable. 'So can you tell me why my co-owner wants to sell up? Your father and I have talked to her but he's as baffled as I am. She's very abrupt on the phone, I must say. Just like a businessman with something to hide, in my experience.'

Holly was just formulating a reply when Rowena beat her to it. 'She's always like that, Mr Longwood, always. Makes snap decisions over everything. She brought us a horse one day and took it away the next. Just said she'd changed her mind and that was it. Dad calls her a real autocrat. I had to look that up in the dictionary and it means an absolute boss in everything with no thought for anybody else. That fits Mrs Bedale like a skull cap.'

They all laughed at that and Holly shot a grateful glance at Ro. It was obvious that Fitzroy Longwood approved of her. She began to think things would turn out well after all.

'I think I can accept that,' Mr Longwood, eyes still twinkling, acknowledged. 'But what of the future? You know as well as I do that racehorses cost a lot of money to keep in training and I'm not made of the stuff. I've already made a substantial investment in Puzzle and I need to see some return on that – some prizemoney, some real promise for the future. Holly, I'm not being hard-hearted, I like my horses very much, but I'm also a businessman.'

'Puzzle *has* got a good future, a great future,' Holly told him as fervently as she could. 'That's not just my opinion. Ray Cable – you must know him: the bookmaker – well he says Puzzle was ridden just for speed at Covenham, that he still improved hurdle by hurdle and that he'll make up into a really good horse one day.'

'Oh, talk to bookies, do we?' inquired Mr Longwood, his eyebrows rising with real or mock surprise. But Holly could tell he was impressed. 'How did he come to confide his views on my horse to you?'

So Holly told him, but only after swearing him to secrecy about her visit to the office in Pier Street. She still didn't know whether the bookmaker might have broken a law in admitting her to his shop to watch a race. Then, daringly, she added: 'I really think Mr Cable'd like a share in Puzzle himself.'

The eyebrows remained aloft while Mr Longwood chewed the inside of his lip. 'Ah, well, I'm not sure that would be a good idea,' he murmured eventually. 'Can't have a bookie walking off with half my prizemoney. Those fellas do well enough out of me as it is!'

Holly recognized that this was the moment to press home the advantage she was sure she'd gained. 'Well,

I know that Vanessa also would like a share in Puzzle. She's even willing to spend her compensation money on him. And – I'd sacrifice all my pocket money for years to come if I could own even a tiny part of him. I mean that, Mr Longwood, with all my heart!'

'Holly, I don't doubt that for a moment,' Fitzroy Longwood responded with the warmest of smiles. 'I think I can recognize devotion when I see it. Well, between you, you've convinced me that I should be the one to buy out Stephanie Bedale's half-share and have Puzzle all to myself. But I promise to make sure you share in his future successes, Holly. How d'you feel about that, eh?'

For once Holly really didn't know what to say. Her first instinct was to rush across to give him a kiss and a hug of gratitude. But she thought that might be over-doing it (in fact, she was wrong: it would have been greatly appreciated). So she simply told him: 'That's just wonderful, *wonderful*. Honestly, I don't know how to thank you enough.'

Now he was positively beaming. 'Just keep looking after the horse the way you have been doing. Then he'll always be ready to run the race of his life. Now, I know what you think about his talent for jumping fences rather than hurdles. So let's get down to discussing some plans for his future . . .'

SEVEN

It was by several degrees the warmest spring day of the year so far. Holly discarded her blue-and-white wool sweater long before she began to lead Puzzle round and round the parade ring at Covenham Racecourse, before the start of the Eckington Hill Novices' Steeplechase for five-year-olds and upwards, over two-and-a-half miles.

On each circuit she exchanged smiles and sometimes a quip with Rowena, who was again staying with the Hill family so that she could be present when Puzzle made his début over fences under National Hunt rules, Ro having told everyone at Hazelton Manor that she wasn't going to miss this event 'for the world!' On this occasion, though, Holly's closest attention was directed at the other eight runners now circling the paddock, accompanied by their own lads and lasses. In the sunlight, coats carried a summer gleam and there wasn't one horse that didn't look in prime condition and ready to run the race of its life. Holly's high hopes for Puzzle's success were beginning to dwindle. How could he be certain to beat such beautiful, fit and – in the case of the leading fancies, Casco Sound and I'll Tell You – much more experienced horses? And if he failed, probably Fitzroy Longwood would want to sell him as soon as possible to cut his losses. In spite of all his kind words to her, Mr Longwood was, as her father regularly reminded her, a businessman,

70

someone who wanted to make a profit out of everything, including his racing.

'Puzzle, you've GOT to win today, GOT to!' she urged under her breath when she was sure no one could hear her. 'Don't let me down, *please!*'

His ears twitched back and forth as they always did when she used her special voice.

A few minutes later her father and Mr Longwood entered the paddock with other owners and trainers and, just as everyone else did, they turned immediately to study their own horse. Holly knew they'd be assessing their chances of winning, but there was nothing she could tell them they couldn't judge for themselves. Puzzle was walking with his customary confident, athletic stride, easily (in her eyes) the best mover of all the runners. He looked lean and healthy and ready to run for his life: and he was.

If only, she reflected for the umpteenth time, she were riding him herself in this race: but that, of course, was impossible. She was too young to ride against professional jockeys and experienced amateur riders in a race of this calibre. At least she could comfort herself with the thought that Billy Wooldale wouldn't be in the saddle. Her father and Mr Longwood had agreed that a change of jockeyship was desirable and so they'd engaged Joshua Hobson, one of the most promising of the current crop of younger riders. His own stable hadn't a runner in the race and so he'd been free to take the ride on Puzzle. Now, as he came into the paddock and touched his blue-and-white quartered cap to owner and trainer and then shook hands with them, Holly darted a quick glance at him. Like Puzzle himself, he had a jaunty stride and a hint of superiority (or was it just confidence?) in his manner. All she could do now was hope they'd take to each other and become a formidable partnership.

The hand-bell was rung and the order given by an official in the ring: 'Jockeys please mount.'

Automatically, Holly turned her horse from the circular path on to the grass and stroked his nose as trainer, jockey and owner came to meet them. The smiles had faded now; the serious business of racing was about to take place.

After murmurings of 'Good luck' and 'I'll do my best, sir' and 'Come back safe and sound', Paddy Hill gave Joshua a leg-up into the saddle. Holly, holding Puzzle's head, wondered what the jockey was really feeling about this ride: was Puzzle going to be special to him or just another mount who'd simply boost his earnings through another riding fee?

'How will this one go, then?' Joshua inquired to Holly's surprise, as she led them towards the gate on to the track. Often enough, jockeys didn't deign to talk to stable lasses they didn't know.

'Oh, he'll win,' she replied without hesitation.

'They all say that,' Joshua laughed. 'Stable girls always think their own horses are future Grand National winners. They soon learn otherwise.'

'You'll see – just keep him up with the pace at the front.'

'Hey, I take my instructions from the trainer, not his lass,' Joshua pointed out, plainly miffed. He urged Puzzle into a canter and Holly was unable to give her horse a farewell pat.

Rowena was waiting to rejoin her and they went to watch the race from a miniature stand reserved for stable lads quite close to the running rail. 'Nobody's going to object to you being here,' Holly assured her when Ro wondered aloud whether she was trespassing. 'You're with me – and I need a bit of moral support today, Ro. I've just told the jockey Puzzle WILL win. I think I'll shoot myself if he doesn't, if anything horrible happens out there.'

Rowena squeezed her arm. 'It's going to be all right. *I* feel it, too. Puzzle looks terrific, never better. You and your dad and Vanessa have turned him into a real racehorse. Anyone can see that.'

As the nine horses milled around at the start and then formed a fairly ragged line, Holly's stomach was still churning furiously with anxiety, her fingers crossing and uncrossing, her tongue flickering between her lips. Watching, she would admit to anyone, was far, far harder than riding. Thankfully, though, her worries couldn't reach Puzzle: the sleek grey appeared to be the calmest horse in the field – and when the starting tape sprang aside, he surged into action as if he'd been waiting all his life for this moment.

Clearly his jockey, having absorbed Patrick Hill's advice, was happy to set the pace. There was a longish run to the first fence but when he reached it Puzzle, standing off, soared over it with such style that there were audible gasps of admiration in the stands. Already the grey wes several lengths ahead of the rest of the field, which was reduced by one when the last runner to approach the obstacle hesitated, made a half-hearted attempt to climb over it and pitched his rider off sideways.

Even before reaching the second fence, an open ditch, Puzzle had increased his advantage over his nearest pursuer, Casco Sound, a very dark bay and the second favourite in the betting. Another prodigious leap caused many in the crowd to consult racecards to check on the leader, a horse who hadn't previously entered their calculations because he was a complete outsider with no known form. Even at 20–1 Holly hadn't bet on him: she was concerned only

73

with his performance, not his price. And, at the moment, that performance was breathtaking.

'He's terrific, terrific!' Ro exclaimed excitedly. 'He's just out there *enjoying* himself.'

Holly didn't speak. Wide-eyed, she was watching his every stride for he was jumping even better than she'd believed possible. He'd shown before that he liked Covenham and that was why they'd brought him back; but now he was apparently revelling in this racecourse. Joshua, letting him have his head but still watchful, was unconcerned about building up so substantial a lead. He sensed that Puzzle wasn't going to run out of steam on this flattish oval, even with more than a mile still to cover. The horse was giving him an awesome feeling of power.

By now, rival jockeys were worrying about their prospects if they hadn't already despaired of them. Casco Sound's rider shook him up in an effort to reduce the gap, but that so unsettled the bay he misjudged the fourth fence completely and paid the penalty by crumpling up on landing. Now only two of the other runners, Beam of Light and the favourite, I'll Tell You, had any hope at all of catching the runaway leader. Then Beam of Light, having his first outing over fences, demonstrated his lack of experience when trying to jump the fifth obstacle while still half-a-length behind the favourite: an error that inevitably brought about his downfall, too.

'Don't look round, just keep going!' Holly, speaking at last, exhorted Joshua. She knew that so long as he didn't relax and therefore risk committing a monumental blunder, they were going to win by 'a distance', the biggest recognizable margin in racing. I'll Tell You, a handsome light chestnut, was jumping well and staying on, but he needed the speed of a champion sprinter to catch Puzzle now.

Joshua didn't relax – and the horse jumped brilliantly and galloped relentlessly to the finishing line. It was, by any reckoning, a scintillating victory.

'Oh, wonderful, wonderful, *wonderful*!' Rowena yelled, flinging her arms around Holly for an exchange of hugs and kisses before they dashed headlong towards the gate to welcome back their hero.

Soon Holly and Fitzroy Longwood and Paddy Hill were submerged by people who wanted to congratulate them: and even the racing journalists almost had to fight a way through to the trainer to ask about future plans for this 'exciting newcomer to steeple-chasing'. Holly was in a state of utter bliss as she listened to Joshua, grinning from ear to ear, tell owner and trainer: 'He just insisted on doing it his way, I did hardly anything. Any time you want me to ride him again, just say the word, *please*. I tell you, I think this is one heck of a good horse.'

Paddy Hill, smiling just as happily, caught his younger daughter's eye as he replied with admirable calm: 'I reckon you could be right. He certainly is One Very Good Horse.'